You are
Brave!

Love -
Gracie
Brave

Gracie Brave

By Pamela Krikke & Kate Eldean MA, MFT

Illustrated by
Jane Moore Houghton

Kate Eldean
xoxo

Published by Mindstir Media LLC

45 Lafayette Rd. Suite 181 | North Hampton, NH 03862 | USA

1.800.767.0531 | www.mindstirmedia.com

Printed in the United States of America

ISBN-13: 978-0-9996085-2-4

Library of Congress Control Number: 2017917164

For all the children of the world and adults that are children at heart.
I AM GRACIE BRAVE AMBASSADOR OF LOVE.
Hello world here I am!

Hi, I'm Gracie Brave and I have a story to tell you. I love hearts.
Any kind of heart. Heart rocks, heart shaped clouds, heart jewels,
heart stickers and heart shapes on my clothes. I love hearts because
they remind me of love.

I love my Ellie the elephant. He makes my heart happy. But what I really like are caterpillars, rainbows, butterflies and going fishing with my Grandpa.

Not long ago I was feeling sad. I wanted to stay in my bedroom where I feel safe. I would rather be playing with my friends, but I did not feel good. You know, like when your tummy aches. When I am this way I like to talk to Dr. Benjamin. He helps me feel better. When I talk to him he teaches me ways that I can help myself when I am having a hard day. He helps me understand my feelings and why I feel sad and alone sometimes.

My Moms name is Claire. She loves me no matter what. She said, Gracie, we need an adventure. Let's go visit Grandma and take that road trip we have been wanting to go on.

This is Ellie. He is my best friend. He goes with me everywhere.
When I am feeling scared, he helps me feel safe.

My Grandma lives far away. I miss her. I was frightened to take my first airplane ride, but I was happy to see my Grandma again. My Mom said, let's sing our brave song.

Take a risk your courage will grow.
Catch those thoughts and let them go.
Take a breath, don't be afraid.
Small step forward Gracie Brave.

Grandma met us at the airport. I was so happy to see her.

She said, Gracie, you are growing so tall!

I got in the back seat of her big, green Cadillac and we headed to San Francisco. There were the biggest trees I have ever seen before.

We stayed in a big hotel. The first night I was scared. The wind was howling and there were shadows on the walls. I held my tummy, hugged Ellie and said, you are brave.

The man at the front desk said, you must be Gracie Brave. He gave me a heart shaped balloon. He told me that it has magical powers if I believe.

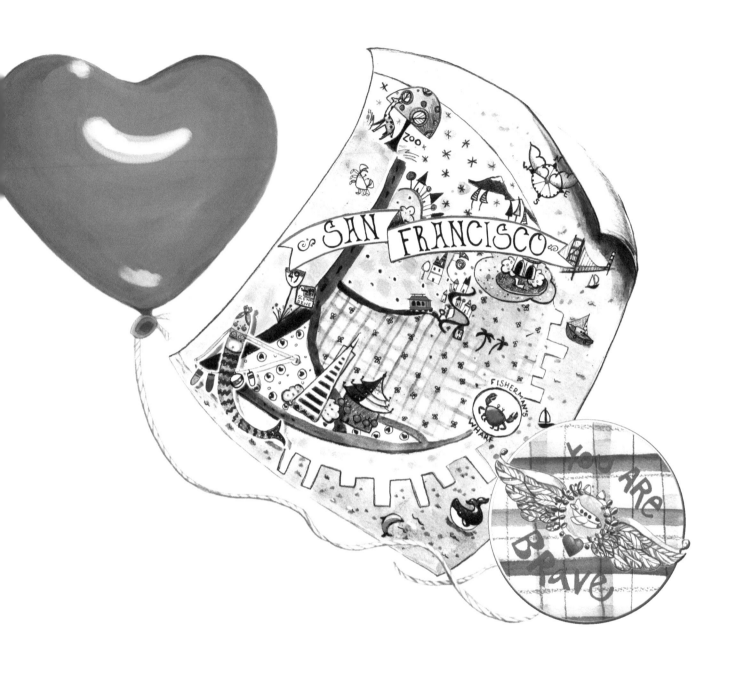

He also gave me this map for all the special places to explore.

The next morning we were off to San Francisco. I wasn't sure about those tall buildings. Dr. Benjamin taught me that when I get nervous to close my eyes and imagine good things.

I closed my eyes and believed in the magic of the balloon. I am a small child, but I have big ideas. My imagination can take me anywhere. Watch me go!

I imagine flying like those birds. They are free and not afraid.

My Mom tells me that my dreams will take me to amazing places.
Even when I don't feel well she believes in me.

I can soar like my magical balloon. I love to run and feel the wind on my face. Watch me go! My heart was feeling very brave.

There were kites flying and children were playing in the park.
There were birds, squirrels, dogs and babies in strollers.

There were so many children in the park. I met a new friend, his name is Wesley Banks. He said that no one wanted to play with him because he stutters.

I told him that I am different too. I want to be liked even when I am grumpy or sad. I know that I am still loved and so are you.

We can go on adventures together and visit children in far away places. Your compass will help us find our way.

Close your eyes and imagine a magical, red balloon that can take us anywhere we want to go. Come with me, we will soar!

Where ever we go we will find children of all colors, shapes and sizes.

Let's join hands and march together. We are all special, just love one another.

We can touch the clouds and watch the world spin around! Come with me!

Gracie, where will our balloon go? Anywhere our imagination takes us.

Gracie you are one of a kind. On your journey, you will find. All the children in the world are one of a kind. Spread your love around the world. You are the one and only ever you.

it's ok to let me soar...

Gracie Go Oh Go
Go out to see the world
Where ever you go, be brave
Shine your light along the way

Resources

Depression is one of the mental disorders that can appear during childhood and adolescence. Today 1 in 33 school-aged children and 1 in 8 adolescents suffers from clinical depression. This resource guide is designed to provide you with information about childhood depression. It will help you recognize the signs and symptoms of depression in your child and what you can do to act on your concerns.

If one of more of these symptoms is present, parents should seek help.

+ Frequent sadness, tearfulness, crying
+ Decreased interest in activities; or inability to enjoy previously favorite activities
+ Hopelessness
+ Persistent boredom; low energy
+ Social isolation, poor communication
+ Low self esteem and guilt
+ Extreme sensitivity to rejection or failure
+ Increased irritability, anger, or hostility
+ Difficulty with relationships
+ Frequent complaints of physical illnesses such as headaches and stomach aches
+ Frequent absences from school or poor performance in school
+ Poor concentration
+ A major change in eating and/or sleeping patterns
+ Talk of or efforts to run away from home
+ Thoughts or expressions of suicide or self destructive behavior

Below are a few suggestions to help you connect with your child.

~Help them understand their feelings:
Give them reassurance that you will help them in any way possible.
Make sure they know they are in a safe place to share their thoughts and feelings regardless of what they are.

~Reading together forms a bond and gives children a sense of intimacy and well-being.
It helps them feel loved, safe and secure. It can relieve stress and anxiety and help with coping skills.

~Ask questions. Come at the depression from a place of curiosity and openness.

Related Websites~

https://www.aacap.org
American Academy of Child and Adolescent Psychiatry

www.nami.org
National Alliance on Mental Illness

KidsHealth.org
KidsHealth is an award-winning website produced by the Nemours Foundation, one of the largest nonprofit organizations devoted to children's health.

We hope that these resources will be helpful on your journey towards more hope and healing.

~Team Gracie Brave

About the Authors

Pam Krikke Writer/Author:

It has been a life long mission to help children, families, and educators how to protect and teach children core values that will give them the tools to have confidence, and strengthen self esteem. Teach them while they are young.

Pam has worked in the field of interior decorating for 34 years. Her other interests include gardening, cooking, flower arranging, golfing and loving on her grandchildren.

Kate Eldean:

Kate Eldean is a licensed Marriage and Family Therapist with over 17 years of experience working with individuals, couples and families in a variety of settings. Kate finds inspiration every day all around her towards pushing towards the feat of being Brave-in the children she counsels, in her friends and family and of course in her own pursuit of Bravery. In her spare time Kate loves boating, arts and crafts, traveling, shopping and cross-cultural ministry in Africa. Kate lives in Charleston, SC with her therapy dog, Josiah. For more information, please visit her website at www.kateeldean.com.